This edition ©Ward Lock Limited 1989

First published in the United States
in 1990 by Gallery Books,
an imprint of W.H. Smith Publishers, Inc.,
112 Madison Avenue, New York 10016.

Gallery Books are available for bulk purchase for sales
promotions and premium use. For details write or telephone
the Manager of Special Sales, W.H. Smith Publishers, Inc.,
112 Madison Avenue, New York, New York 10016. (212) 532-6600.

ISBN 0-8317-0968-5

Printed and bound in Hungary

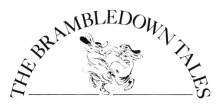

THE BRAMBLEDOWN TALES

YELLOW DUCKLING'S STORY

GALLERY BOOKS

An Imprint of W. H. Smith Publishers Inc.

112 Madison Avenue

New York, New York 10016

Yellow Duckling wanted to *live!*

Chapter One

COME ALIVE

Between the clean clouds and the green ground, with trees and hills all around, stands Brambledown. You know it, don't you? I expect you've seen, in the far distance, the sun glinting on Pease Pond and smoke rising up from the chimney pots.

Who wants to stay inside when the sun is shining, when you can hear people playing outside and the river trickling and the birds singing and hurrying footsteps going to and fro? Not Yellow Duckling! She wanted to go out and see the Big World. She wanted to see all these wonders for herself. She wanted to *live*! But what could she do? She was only a felt shape sewn on a cushion in the window of Hayseed Cottage. And cushions can't go out, can they?

Away went Yellow

The funny thing is, that it was not a sunny day at all when Yellow's dream came true. On the contrary, the wind was rattling the windows and now and then it rained. It was a bad day for Mrs Hayseed to get her washing dry and ready to be ironed.

Oh it was the middle of summer. But what a summer! From one week to the next, the sun did not show herself. The rain kept raining and the wind kept blowing grimy dark clouds across the sky like a flock of grubby sheep.

But Mrs Hayseed had done her washing – the curtains and cloths and clothes and even the cushion cover where Yellow Duckling sat stitched. Yellow did not like being washed, but she liked being hung on the washline to dry in the wind. But today was different.

The wind pulled and jerked at the square of cloth and suddenly – *click*! – the pegs flew off and away went Yellow.

Over the fence and over the hedges blew the clean cushion cover, across the road and down the lane. "Oh! Oh! Oh!" cried Yellow as the mud dirtied her yellow felt wings. "I know I wanted to see the world but this is a very rough way to travel!"

At last the cushion cover came to rest in among reeds at the edge of Pease Pond. At any moment it might tumble into the water and sink down to the muddy bottom and never be found. And Yellow could not move a feather or a foot.

But was she frightened? Not a bit of it! She was much too full of wonder at seeing the sloppy water, the rustling reeds and all the reflections in the pond. "This is the place for a duck to be!" she cried. "If only I were alive I would wriggle off this cushion and dabble my feet in that water!"

On the grass nearby, a thrush was singing.

"Oh how I wish I could open my beak and quack!" thought Yellow.

Overhead, a pigeon flew by.

"Oh if only I could spread my wings and flap!" thought Yellow.

Thrush was singing

The cover slipped down a little further. "Oh dear. It seems as if I must just sink into the water and drown. Ah well. At least just once I've seen a real pond and real birds, too. I mustn't complain . . . Oh look! A beautiful butterfly! How lucky I am!" And the cover slipped down even further and dipped one corner in the muddy water.

Now the butterfly was out on patrol. She was a helper of the Guardian Water Sprite, and she flew off to tell her master about the strange Thing that had blown to his pond.

She described the cushion cover and the yellow felt duckling sewn there.

"So *that's* who I heard wishing!" said the Water Sprite. He sprang onto his mount – a bright blue dragonfly with whirring wings – and flew to the rescue. Butterfly led the way, and the Sprite was just in time to save the cushion cover from sinking beneath the muddy water.

"Hello little duckling! Are you quite comfortable sitting there?"

Yellow was not used to people speaking to her. Mostly people thought of her as just a felt shape. "Quite comfortable, thank you, sir. Of course I would love to stretch out my wings and fly and swim and waddle and quack . . . but I'm only a felt shape."

"A felt shape, indeed!" cried the Sprite. "A duckling's what you are and a duckling's what you shall be!"

A beautiful butterfly

"Just for today!"

Chapter Two

BAD WEATHER BLUES

With a word of magic and a wave of his hand, the Guardian Water Sprite sprinkled a few drops of water over Yellow Duckling. First she felt a most peculiar tickling under the wings, and then she sneezed –

Atchooo!

And do you know what? She sneezed herself clean off the cushion. There she stood in yellow feathers and orange feet – a real duckling from her beak to her yellow tail! A duckling newly come alive.

"Just for today!" said the Sprite leaping back onto his dragonfly. "But stay near the Pond. The Big World is a dangerous place! And don't be surprised if you don't like it quite as much as you suppose! Don't forget now, it's just for today. Make the most of it!"

You never saw such a happy little duck! She launched herself into the pond with a big splash, and rolled on the blowy waves, and paddled her orange feet. "Oh thank you, Mr Sprite, sir! You can't know how I've longed to swim about and flap my wings. Oh thank you! Thank you! I shall love every minute!"

*S*nooty *B*ee

"Buzz buzz! Watch who you're splashing, you clumsy creature! Look what you've done now! You've made me drop some of the pollen I was carrying!"

"Sorry, sorry, sorry!" said Yellow to the snooty Bee. "It's just that I'm so happy. It's so good to be alive! I just couldn't help splashing."

"How zz-illy! What nonzzenzze?" buzzed the Bee. "How can anyone by happy in *thiz* weather? The flowers won't open properly and everywhere iz too wet for me to land."

"Oh dear. I hadn't noticed," said Yellow apologetically. "You see, I've only just come to life and everything looks so very wonderful to me – the raindrops glistening on the grass like diamonds and flowers dancing in the wind."

But the snooty Bee buzzed on his way, too bad-tempered to notice such things.

Yellow ducked her head below the water and tugged at some silkweed. It was the most delicious thing she had ever tasted in her life . . . but then it was the *first* thing she had ever tasted.

After that she practised balancing on her nose with her tail in the air. What fun it was! The wind blowing through the reeds made a sound like music. Yellow blew a few bubbles and ate a worm or two.

"That's right! Eat me out of house and home, with never so much as a please or a thank you!" said a complaining voice. It was Cornelius the Carp.

"Aren't things bad enough, with this filthy weather, without *strangers* coming along and helping themselves to a person's food? Self, self, self – that's all some people think about! It never *used* to be like this."

"Sorry, sorry, sorry!" said Yellow. "I didn't realize that there was a shortage of food in the pond. In fact I didn't know there was anyone else living here, or I would have asked before I took any worms, naturally."

"Huh!" said the Carp pulling an ugly face. "A likely story. Anyway, I haven't seen you before. Who are you?"

"I'm Yellow," said the little duckling brightly. "I've only just come alive. Perhaps that's why I'm so stupid. Oh how I envy you living all your life in such a beautiful place!"

"Beautiful? What's beautiful about it?" demanded Cornelius. "It was beautiful *last* summer, when the sun shone."

And he rolled his fish eyes to the dark sky in despair.

"Ah but see how the wind makes valleys and mountains out of the water," said Yellow gazing about her, "and how the pondweed waves like mermaid-hair . . . Oh and listen to the reeds singing in the morning breeze!"

"Huh!" said Cornelius a second time, turning down the corners of his big mouth. "Don't talk to me about *beautiful*. Last summer was beautiful. You should have been here last summer. Then there was plenty of food in Pease Pond – enough for fish and tadpoles and frogs and coots and *strangers* . . . What an odd shade you are, anyway. So very *yellow*."

"I'm only alive for the day. I'm felt really," said Yellow, but the Carp did not understand.

"I'm fed-up," he said and, with a flick of his tail, plunged deep into the dark waters of Pease Pond.

Cornelius plunged deep

"Bravo! Encore! More, more!"

Chapter Three

WHO WILL BE MAYOR?

"Oh dear, how unhappy everybody seems to be," thought Yellow. "I don't think they find being alive as wonderful as I do."

In fact it felt so wonderful that Yellow had to dance. And when she had danced in the water, she danced on the bank – kicking her webbed feet high in the air and clapping her wingtips and hopping to the music of the wind in the reeds.

The Brown family of rabbits were passing, and they stopped to watch the dancing duck. It was such a happy sight that the Browns began dancing themselves, and when Yellow stopped they cheered and shouted, "Bravo! Encore! More, more!" and clapped their furry paws. For a while they completely forgot about the squabbles in Brambledown.

Splash!

It was too good to last. The bank was muddy and Bud, the smallest rabbit, hopped too high and slithered on the slippery mud – *SPLASH*! into the pond. "Oh! Oh! Oh! Help! Get me out! I'm getting wet!" shrieked Bud.

"Oh my poor baby!" wailed Mrs Brown, wringing her ears. Mr Barney Brown ran up and down the bank. The other little rabbits covered their eyes with their paws in terror.

But Yellow jumped in and rescued Bud. She lifted him out of the water in her beak, and set him gently on the bank.

"Bandeycoots and botheration!" declared Barney stamping his foot. "It's always the same. As soon as we start enjoying ourselves nowadays, something goes wrong."

"Atchoo," said Bud. "I'm c-c-cold, Pa."

"I'm sorry," said Yellow. "It's all my fault. I seem to keep making trouble for people, but I don't mean to. I only came alive this morning and it feels too good for standing still and frowning."

"That's all very well if you're waterproof," said Barney grumpily. "I suppose we had better go home, wife, and dry Bud before he catches cold."

"Why don't you dance Bud dry?" Yellow suggested.

The Browns looked doubtful, but they had to admit that it was a good idea. So they all began dancing. It's hard to dance and to feel unhappy both at once, so the more they danced, the better they all felt. Little Bud dried off, too.

"Dance him dry"

"Who *are* you, stranger?" Barney asked. "You're very *yellow*."

"I was felt this morning, but I'm feathers now," said Yellow.

But Barney was not really listening. He said, "You're a splendid duckling, madam, and I hope you will vote for me in the Election."

"What's that?" said Yellow.

"Why the Choosing of the Mayor, of course! Haven't you heard? The creatures of Brambledown are choosing a Mayor. We must have someone to settle our quarrels."

"But *do* you quarrel?" asked Yellow in amazement. "I heard that Brambledown was the most friendly place in the world!"

"Ah! So it was *last* year," said Barney sadly. "But this year the weather is so bad that the birds bicker and the fish fight and the squirrels squabble and the tiresome tadpoles . . ."

"Leave us out of it, furry face!" came an angry squeak.

"Leave us out of it!"

"G-go on! Hop-op it!"

A tadpole black as rage came to the surface of the pool. "Come up here, Pa! That big fat rabbit Barney Brown called us tiresome tadpoles! Come and box his ears!"

Sure enough, Oggie the Frog leapt out of the Pond onto a flat stone, puffing out his throat for all the world as if he meant to start a fight. "G-go on! Hop-op it, Brown-Clown, before I spit in your eye! Pick on someone your own size if you want to be insulting!"

"I was only saying how your young tadpoles are always complaining lately, and fighting over their food, and . . ."

"G-go on! G-go on! Insult the g-good name of frog-ogs and tadpopples!" cried Oggie. "You'll be sorry when I'm Mayor! Just you wait and see . . ."

"Do you want to be mayor, too?"

Chapter Four

TROUBLE BREWING

"You? Be *Mayor*? Don't make me laugh!" said Barney. "That's a job for a rabbit."

"No it's not! It's a job for a fish," said Cornelius Carp leaping out of the water. "Me!"

"No, me!" said Henry Hedgehog poking his nose through the reeds.

"No, me!" said Maurice the Mole popping up out of the ground.

"No, me!" cried the Speckled Thrush flying overhead.

"I'm most confused," said Yellow.

Sidney Snail slid down the leaf of a water iris and wagged his horns to beckon the little duckling. "Do *you* want to be Mayor, too?" asked Yellow. "Perhaps you should *all* be Mayors!"

"Peace and quiet"

"I just want some peace and quiet," said Sidney the Snail. "I can smell trouble brewing, then I cannot stop it. You see, I move so slowly. Someone must go to Goodness the Garden Gnome and tell him about all this quarrelling. Everyone is so keen to be Mayor – I'm afraid there will be tears before bedtime – tears and fisticuffs and bruises and nosebleeds. I wouldn't be surprised if there wasn't a *war*."

The awful word made Yellow tremble right down to her orange webbed feet. "Where does Goodness the Gnome live?" she asked.

"Way over yonder – on the edge of the village. Oh it's such a long way over the fields – and so dangerous . . . what with the wicked Weasels and the fiendish Mr Fox and stoats and owls and . . ."

"Now I see what the Sprite meant. It is none too easy being alive," said Yellow. "But I've only got one day, so I must hurry. Goodbye, Mr Snail. Wish me luck!"

"You can't go!" Sidney protested. "It's far too dangerous out there for a little duck." But Yellow was already on her way. Behind her she could hear the voices of the animals quarrelling:

"But I'm cleverer than you."

"But fur is always better than feather!"

"Who says? Who says?"

"Everyone knows that water is better than dry land . . ." Soon Yellow was too far away from the Pond to hear the arguing.

Of course, she was very frightened then. "The Sprite said I wasn't to leave the Pond. I do hope he won't be angry."

"Good *evening*," said the Weasel.

"Good *evening*"

"Where did you come from?" asked Yellow with a start.

"I crept up on you," said the wicked Weasel with a wicked grin. "That's what I do. First I creep up and then I pounce on people – like THIS!"

A loud buzzing

But just as the wicked Weasel pounced on Yellow to gobble her up, there was a loud buzzing in his ear. "Oh don't sting me! Get away, you horrible Bee! Don't sting!"

Away ran the Weasel, chased by the Bee, uphill and down dale, into trees and out of them, under bushes and through briars. Buzz buzz buzz.

Soon Yellow was safe to go on her way. The Snail was right – it was a long, long way to Goodness the Gnome's house – all the way through Brambledown Wood and across Farmer Hayseed's field and along the village road. A long walk for a small duckling only newly come alive.

She walked and she waddled until her poor orange feet were quite sore.

She saw the fiendish Mr Fox, but he did not see her. He was too busy pinning posters to the trees:

Vote for Mr Fox!
Mr Fox for Mayor . . . or else!

Just when Yellow thought she must have lost her way, the Bee came buzzing back. "I've chased that wicked Weasel all the way home. But I'll stay with you, in case there are any more like him about."

"You are *very* kind," said Yellow, "especially after I splashed you and made you drop some of your pollen."

"That's all right," said the Bee. "I didn't realize how newly come alive you were. Do you begin to see now how horrible everything is since the sun forgot how to shine? It wasn't like this *last* year."

Yellow looked around her. Yet again it was starting to rain.

So beautiful

The raindrops glistened on the leaves. The petals fell from the dog-roses in the hedge and left the hips gleaming green as emeralds. Even the stones in the muddy road shone and glistened. The wind made the wheat in the fields toss like a golden sea, and the trees seemed to be dancing. Purple clouds sailed like ships across the wild sky, and now and then, a bolt of lightning flashed down out of the clouds, like a golden fork jabbing at a plate of food.

The rain ran down Yellow's back and trickled under all her feathers. She shook her tail and silvery water drops flew in all directions. "I'm sorry, Bee. But I'm afraid I'm just too stupid. It seems like wonderful weather to me. Don't you know that ducks love the rain? It makes me feel like dancing!

"When I was sewed to a cushion cover, and the sun shone in hot through the window, it made my felt fade. I preferred it when it rained and I could watch the raindrops racing each other down the windowpane. Now I'm alive, everything is even more beautiful. Ah! Smell the wet grass. Just smell it!" And she took a deep breath and sighed.

"Zz-illy person!" buzzed the Bee, but he could not help liking Yellow, because she could always find good in everything. And that was unusual in Brambledown this summer!

At last they reached the little cottage on the edge of Brambledown Village. Yellow Duckling waited nervously by the small front door. "I do hope Goodness the Gnome is at home and doesn't mind seeing troublesome visitors like me."

The small front door

"I will tell you how to choose a Mayor"

Chapter Five

BRAMBLEDOWN CHOOSES

"Hello Stranger!" said the little man on the garden path. "And who might you be?" Yellow gabbled out her story. "I'm Yellow, and I'm only alive for one day. I've come from Pease Pond to ask you to help. The animals are quarrelling about who is to be Mayor, and it's all because the sun won't shine and Sidney Snail says it will all end in tears. . . ! Will *you* choose, Mr Gnome? Will you help? *Please*, you're the only one who can!"

Goodness the Gnome put his head on one side and looked at Yellow. "Indeed I will tell them how to choose a Mayor, Yellow Duckling. But do you mean to say you had just one day to be alive and you have spent it coming here? Over the fields and through the woods where the wicked Weasel lives?"

"She did! She did!" buzzed the Bee. And the Butterfly (who was passing) had to agree. "She's a horrible *happy* kind of a duck. Do you know? She even likes the weather!"

"She did! She did!"

Goodness put an arm round Yellow's shoulders. "Let me explain, my good friend. Everybody in Brambledown – except you and me – is bad-tempered and miserable just now. And why? Because the weather is so bad. The rain keeps raining and the sun won't shine and the wind never stops blowing. It's not a very good excuse for being nasty to each other, I know, but there you are. That's the reason."

"It's lovely weather for ducks," said Yellow puzzled, "but I think I understand."

"I want you to go back to the animals and tell them this. Whoever can change the weather for the better deserves to be made the Mayor of Brambledown."

"Won't you come and tell them yourself?" said Yellow in dismay. "They'll never listen to me! I'm only a silly felt Duckling newly come alive!"

"Nonsense! Tell them that I sent you as my special messenger. Tell them that I will be very angry if they don't do as I say," said the Gnome. "Hurry back now. The animals may already be fighting. Or you may turn back into a felt duck before you have delivered my message."

"You're right! You're right!" cried Yellow, and pattered away down the road towards Brambledown Wood as fast as she could go on her sore orange feet. The Bee and Butterfly could hardly keep up with her she went so fast.

Goodness the Gnome went back inside his cottage – but only to fetch his umbrella. Then he, too, set off on a journey of his own, splashing through the puddles and whistling as he went.

Yellow knew when she was getting close to Pease Pond again. She could hear the animals squabbling. The Jay was pecking Sam Squirrel, and the Mole was brandishing his spade and shouting, "I want to be Mayor! Want to! Want to!"

Yellow pattered out from the trees and slithered to a halt on the muddy bank. She rose up on the tips of her webbed feet and wagged her wings: "Listen everybody! I have a message from Goodness the Gnome!"

"Listen everybody!"

"He knows how to choose a Mayor for Brambledown!"

A sudden silence fell over Pease Pond.

"He sent *you*?" said Cornelius Carp, and Yellow blushed a sunny sort of orange.

"I wish everybody could be Mayor, then no-one would be . . ."

"Who's it to be?" interrupted Henry the Hedgehog impatiently.

"Oh. Goodness says the Mayor ought to be the one who can change the weather for the better. Of course I think it's wonderful weather, but I'm only a silly felt duck newly come alive."

Again silence fell. "Who can make the sun shine?" asked Maurice the Mole. "Not me."

"Who can stop the rain?" asked Barney Brown. "Not me."

"Perhaps the fiendish Mr Fox can frighten away the bad weather?" suggested Yellow.

But everyone agreed: "He certainly can't! He can only frighten us!"

"Who can stop the wind blowing?" said Henry the Hedgehog scratching his head. "Not me."

"Who can turn the sky blue when it's dark?" asked Cornelius Carp. "Not me."

"I think I understand what Goodness means," said Sam Squirrel suddenly. "None of us is strong enough to do anything about the weather. So none of us is strong enough to be Mayor of Brambledown."

"Excuse me, but why do you want a Mayor at all?" asked Yellow.

"I understand," said Sam

"Because this awful weather has made us all so bad-tempered, of course," snapped the Jay. "We must have some-one to settle our quarrels. . . . And by the way, Duck, why can't *you* be bad-tempered like everybody else? Eh? Eh? Bah!"

"Yes! What's the matter with *you*!" moaned the other animals.

"I'm so sorry," said Yellow. "It's just that I only have one day to be alive. So I can't say that today is worse than yesterday or better than tomorrow. If *you* only had one day, *you* would probably think today was a lovely day."

Then all the animals turned rather pale. "She only has today," said Sidney Snail. "The sun might shine for us tomorrow, but not for Yellow."

"Eh? Eh? Bah!"

"I forgot it was raining when we were dancing," said Little Bud Brown.

"It's all right for her," grumbled the Jay. "Ducks like the rain."

"But Yellow likes everything," said Bee.

"And Yellow likes everyone," said Henry.

"Even though we are so bad-tempered," said Cornelius Carp. And the animals felt ashamed of themselves, because Yellow was so jolly and they were so grumpy.

"Time to go now, Yellow"

Chapter Six
TIME TO GO

"I think Yellow ought to be Mayor!" said Barney Brown, "because she is so sunny! She would make us all feel warm and happy."

"I'm afraid she won't have time," said a high sweet voice, and the Guardian Water Sprite came in to land on his blue dragonfly. "It's time for Yellow to go back to Hayseed Cottage."

"Ah well. It was very kind of you," said the little duckling, "and I am so glad you've all decided to stop quarrelling."

"Time to go now, Yellow," said the Water Sprite, and he laid the cushion cover flat on the bank of Pease Pond.

"I am rather tired," Yellow admitted, "although it's been a wonderful day – the most wonderful day of my life!"

"I am sorry we didn't make you more welcome," said Barney Brown rabbit.

"I'm sorry you can't stay any longer," said Cornelius Carp.

"I'm sorry you didn't see Pease Pond with the sun shining," said Oggie Frog.

". . . and with the water lilies out . . ."

". . . and the irises in bloom!"

Yellow Duckling bowed low to all her friends. "And I'm sorry I couldn't teach you to like the rain." She sat down in the middle of the cover. The sun was about to go down.

"I hear you left the Pond today," said the Sprite. "After I warned you of all the dangers."

Yellow bowed her head. "I have to admit that I did."

"Goodness the Gnome told me when he came visiting this afternoon.

Sun down

"Goodness told me that you walked all the way to his cottage, to ask his advice."

"I have to admit that I did," replied Yellow.

"And do you know what else he told me, Yellow?" asked the Guardian Water Sprite.

"No, sir. What, sir?"

"That he wants you to come to tea with him often in the future. So! It seems I shall have to send my dragonfly to Hayseed Cottage to be your taxi!"

"But . . . But I . . . I'm only a little felt duck!" quacked Yellow as her feathers and feet and beak turned to cloth, and she settled back onto the cushion cover.

"But once a week you shall be a real duckling and my dragonfly will bring you safely here to Pease Pond – we can't have you meeting a wicked Weasel on the way – and then you shall see the Big World in all kinds of weather . . . though I suppose you will still like it best in the rain. Ducks are funny like that."

A gust of wind – I think it was magic wind – lifted the cushion cover and blew it high over hedge and field and fence. It landed on the lawn of Hayseed Cottage where Mrs Hayseed found it. "Oh dear – this cover has fallen off the washline. But how lucky! It's not even dirty. And how strange! It's quite dry, too, even after all that rain. The duckling shows up very nicely now it is fresh washed. I've always liked this old cushion cover – such a jolly pattern."

The next day the sun came out, and the rain went away, and the wind dropped and the sky was as blue as Pease Pond. All the creatures of Brambledown turned their faces to the warmth of the sun, and happily sunned themselves. Their bad temper and sulks disappeared, like puddles disappearing in the sunshine. They felt particularly happy when they thought about the new friend they had found in Yellow Duckling. And they felt specially happy that she would be back again soon.

And once a week the magic of the Guardian Water Sprite and his spritely dragonfly carried Yellow Duckling to Pease Pond. Not Yellow, that odd felt shape stitched to an old cushion cover in Hayseed Cottage. No, Yellow the real *live* Duckling with bright yellow feathers, dancing orange feet, a quacking orange beak – and the sunniest nature in the whole wide world, come rain or shine!

Such a jolly pattern